The pig on the hill

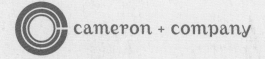
cameron + company

**To my wife Cathy,
the Duck Whisperer**

The pig on the hill
All text and illustration
© 2013 John Kelly

Library of Congress Control
Number: 2013932040

ISBN: 978-1-937359-39-3

Printed and bound in China

10 9 8 7 6 5 4 3 2 1

 cameron + company

Petaluma Blvd. North
Suite B6
Petaluma
CA 94952

(707) 769-1617
www.cameronbooks.com

The pig on the hill

John Kelly

Pig lived on the hill.

The views were amazing.

He was very fond of cooking (especially cakes).

He dabbled with models and did jigsaw puzzles.

He liked to keep busy.

His life was perfect.

Until one morning
when he opened
his curtains.

"Good morning!", said the duck.
"Beautiful day, isn't it?"

Pig agreed, but secretly
wished the duck would
just go away.

He was spoiling the view.

"Such a marvelous spot!
You can see for miles."

Pig watched the duck.

He seemed to be
taking notes.

Eventually he flew off,
and Pig breathed
a sigh of relief.

But the very next morning the duck was back.

"I'm going to build a house here," he said.
"It's just such a marvelous spot."

Over the next
few days there
was hammering,
sawing, banging,
scraping, drilling.

The duck even had
a swimming pool
delivered.

Pig tried his best to ignore
the disruption, and eventually...

...the duck's house
was finished.

There was a
knock at the door.

"Hi there, neighbor!"
said the duck.

Pig had no choice
but to let him in.

His new neighbor
was full of stories.

The duck
seemed to
have been
everywhere
and done
everything.

Things Pig had only
read about in books.

Pig thought the duck
was a bit of a show-off.

And was glad when
he finally went home.

As spring turned to summer
Pig saw more and more of
his new neighbor.

There were the normal disagreements.

But they discovered some common interests.

And, like all good neighbors, they helped each other out.

Especially in moments of crisis.

Summer turned to fall.

And before long it was winter.

One morning Pig woke to find Duck had built a bridge between their two houses.

"I thought I'd make it easier for you to pop over," said Duck.

"Since you can't fly."

"By the way, I'm having a party tonight. Will you come?"

But Pig didn't like crowds.

So he said no.

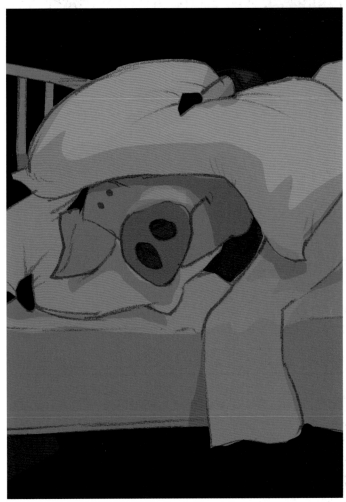

Pig tried to sleep.

But the music seemed to go on and on and on and on.

In the end Pig couldn't stand it anymore!

He stomped across the
bridge to Duck's house.

"WILL YOU PLEASE BE QUIET?"

The party stopped.

"I'm very sorry," said Duck.

He sent all of his
guests home at once.

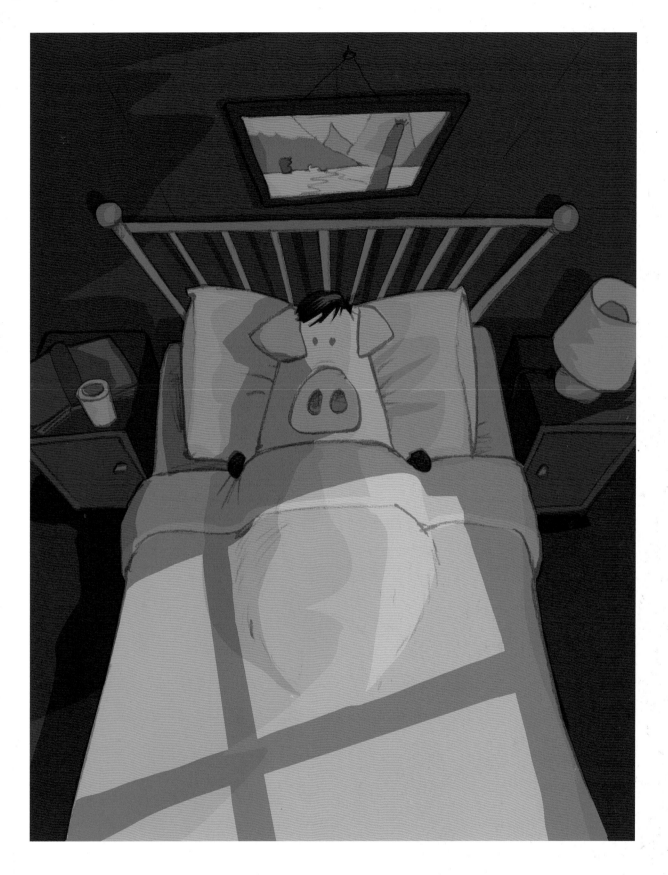

Pig went back to bed. But he couldn't sleep.

He felt very bad for spoiling Duck's party.

In the morning he crossed the bridge again, to apologize.

But there was no one home.

Duck didn't return that day.

Or the next.

Or the next.

As the weather grew colder
there was still no sign of
his neighbor.

Pig's own house fell quiet once again.

Just like it had been
before Duck arrived.

Soon it was
spring again.

But Duck's house
was still silent
and empty.

Then one day there was
a knock at Pig's door.

"Buenos dias, neighbor!"

Duck was back!

He explained that every year,
when it got too cold, he flew off...

...somewhere nice and warm.

Duck brought presents back from his holiday.

Soon things were
back to normal.

That year, Pig decided he didn't want to spend winter alone again.

So he had an idea.

And the next time Duck went on holiday...

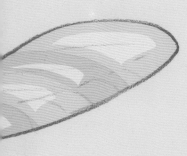

Pig went too.

Thanks to Iain, Chris, Nina and everyone
at Cameron for their faith – J.K.

CAMERON + COMPANY
Publisher: Chris Gruener
VP Children's: Nina Gruener
Art Direction & Design: Iain R. Morris
Editor: Amy Novesky

(707) 769–1617
www.cameronbooks.com